MW00748455

The Little Gift Book of

BRITISH COLUMBIA

The Little Gift Book of

BRITISH COLUMBIA

Whitecap Books
Vancouver / Toronto

Whitecap Books
Vancouver / Toronto

Text by Darby Macnab
Edited by Linda Ostrowalker
Cover and interior design by Carolyn Deby

Typography by CompuType, Vancouver, B.C., Canada

Printed and bound in Canada by D.W. Friesen and Sons Ltd., Altona, Manitoba

CANADIAN CATALOGUING IN PUBLICATION DATA

Macnab, Darby
The little gift book of British Columbia

ISBN 1-895099-38-2

1. British Columbia - Description and travel - 1981 - Views. I. Title.

FC3817.4.M25 1991 971.1′04′0222 C91-091068-5
F1087.M25 1991

Cover: Sunrise at Long Beach, Pacific Rim National Park, on Vancouver Island
Bob Herger

Contents

Sailboats moored at Coal Harbour in downtown Vancouver.

British Columbia

British Columbia, Canada's westernmost province, is a land of dramatic beauty. From the Continental Divide high atop the Rocky Mountains, headwaters tumble westward, building into enormously powerful rivers which course overland toward the Pacific Ocean. Waves of mountain ranges undulate across the interior, and long, narrow lakes lie wedged between them in glacier-formed nooks and crannies. Ancient rain forests flourish in valleys near the coast, while evergreen forests blanket huge portions of the province, giving way only to cultivated farmlands and to the grasslands of the central plateaus. In the west, the massive Coast Mountains loom over menacing ocean waters, as waves beat relentlessly at the craggy fjords below. And off the southwest coast, Vancouver Island acts as a barrier against Pacific storms, and a gentler ocean laps at the perimeters of the province's two largest cities, Victoria and Vancouver.

The grandeur of British Columbia's natural beauty has staggered newcomers for centuries. Late 18th-century explorers discovered here a world of superlatives — some of the highest mountains, the oldest trees, the most powerful rivers, the most sophisticated native Indian cultures lay within this

Left: *Wave backwash, south beach, Pacific Rim National Park.*

unexplored realm. Then, as now, the sea, mountains, rivers, lakes, and forests dominated the land, molding it, influencing settlement patterns and economic development.

Once, the native Indian peoples here were as varied as the regions they inhabited, from the salmon and cedar oriented coastal tribes, to the hunters and gatherers of the interior plateaus. The loss, through disease and destruction, of these native cultures was one of the earliest and most profound of corruptions cast by the Europeans upon this new territory.

Ever since fur-trading claims were staked out 200 years ago, man has been dipping into nature's generous stores here, and the province's boom and bust economy has grown strong on forestry, mining, fishing and agriculture, as well as tourism, which today is British Columbia's second largest industry.

Despite its natural-resource-based prosperity, there remain vast expanses of untainted wilderness within British Columbia's borders. In the northern half of the province, boreal forest, muskeg and alpine tundra stretch for hundreds of kilometres, towns are rare, and connections to the south are limited. Meanwhile the fertile and populous south holds well over half of the province's 3 million people, but even here the great outdoors are never far away, and the recreational opportunities are never less than spectacular.

People from all over the world have made British Columbia their home — including many Canadians who have crossed the Rockies and never looked back. There is a shared sense of identity amongst the people of this province — a tradition of celebrating and respecting their natural inheritance — that bodes well for the future of this favoured land.

Shriners' Parade at the Pacific National Exhibition.

Lower Mainland

Lured by the natural beauty of British Columbia, many visitors are surprised to find a large, sophisticated city perched on the shores of the Pacific in the province's southwest corner. In fact, Vancouver and its environs has a population of over 1.5 million people, making it Canada's third largest metropolis. With the rhythm of the tides lapping at its edges, and the majestic Coast Mountains watching over it, Vancouver is one of the most alluring of North American cities.

As the province's commercial and industrial heart, Vancouver has grown from a sawmill shantytown at the beginning of the century to a vibrant and stylish city. When it hosted Expo '86, hundreds of thousands of visitors discovered it to be a world-class city with a difference. Shops and restaurants with an international flavour dot the downtown core, while unparalleled recreation and sporting opportunities, such as hiking, skiing, camping, fishing, sailing, windsurfing and scuba diving, are literally only minutes away.

As Canada's gateway to the Pacific Rim, Vancouver enjoys a staggering prosperity. Every day, giant freighters from myriad countries glide through English Bay into Vancouver's port — third largest in North America —

Left: *Alex Fraser Bridge spans the south arm of the Fraser River.*

with terminals handling everything from coal and petroleum, to forest and agricultural products and minerals. And to the south, the mighty Fraser River thrives with logging and fishing activity.

Balancing out the hustle and bustle, however, is the resort-town air that descends each summer, when residents and visitors alike come out to play on the city's sandy beaches and in its forested parks. There is a gentleness to the pulse of this city, and a softness to its temperate climate that combine to make Vancouver a most livable place.

Winter, too, holds its delights, especially for those who take the 1½ hour drive up the coast to Whistler — now an internationally renowned ski resort. Those who do enjoy some of the finest coastal scenery anywhere, as the highway skirts past dazzling, fjord-like inlets, then winds through the deep green forests, by plunging waterfalls, and around soaring, snow-capped peaks of "sea-to-sky country."

To the northwest lies the Sunshine Coast, aptly named, as it receives over 2,400 hours of sunshine annually — more even than Hawaii. Here are some of the world's best fishing, diving and boating waters. Exotic marine life, ancient shipwrecks, and, of course, the rich history of the Salish Indians all combine to make this area a popular vacationing spot.

To the east of Greater Vancouver, Fraser Valley Heritage Country holds the secrets of this region's early settlement history, most notably, Fort Langley, which stands as it was built in 1827 as a Hudson's Bay Company fur-trading post. Still further east, provincial parks and peaceful rural communities slowly give way to the lush farmlands of the Fraser Valley. This is one of Canada's prime agricultural areas, where the shimmering summer heat brings forth fresh fruits, vegetables, nuts, and honey, and where dairy farms and nurseries thrive. As the Fraser River flows, so does the harvest, towards the hub of the province at the mouth of this river.

Canada Place in Vancouver's downtown core.

Frontyard gardens in a Kitsilano neighbourhood.

Crisp fall colours in Crescent Park.

A bustling market shop in Vancouver's Chinatown.

The original General Store at Fort Langley, built in 1827.

The bright lights of Chinatown at night.

Farmland near Yarrow, deep in the Fraser Valley.

The original Hastings Mill Store, built in 1865.

Orcas performing at the Vancouver Aquarium in Stanley Park.

Sheltered moorings at Deep Cove in North Vancouver.

Vancouver's Art Gallery, formerly the Court House.

Distant mountain ranges greet a skier at Cypress Bowl near Vancouver.

Sailing at Alta Lake, near Whistler Mountain Ski Resort.

Simon Fraser University, perched atop Burnaby Mountain.

A view of Diamond Head from one of the Elphin Lakes.

The rocky promontory of Lighthouse Park in West Vancouver.

Tulips abound at Fantasy Gardens in Richmond.

Pitt Meadows on the banks of the Pitt River.

The Coast Mountains, shrouded in clouds and blanketed by glaciers.

Vancouver Island

The largest Pacific island off of North America, Vancouver Island is a study in contrasts. Its weather-beaten west coast withstands the ravages of ocean storms almost all year round, while the ridge of mountains running down the island's centre protects the eastern lowlands, where fields and pastures roll gently toward the sea. Sheltered between Vancouver Island's southeast coast and the mainland lie the green and fertile Gulf Islands, and to the north is a maze of islands and mainland fjords where tidal rapids occur in dangerous channels that challenge today's yachtsmen just as they did the explorers of yesteryear.

The force of the Pacific has carved countless narrow inlets in Vancouver Island's west coast, where tenacious wind-blown trees cling to cliff tops and communities are rare and remote. The hardy people of these outposts share the sea with a variety of native marine mammals, from Steller's sea lions, sea otters, dolphins and seals, to the legendary Orcas, or killer whales.

When Captain George Vancouver encountered the island on his way up the mainland coast in 1793, he remarked on "the serenity of the climate,

Left: *Butchart Gardens on Vancouver Island, created from an abandoned limestone quarry.*

the innumerable pleasing landscapes and the abundant fertility that nature puts forth." Yet, on the far side of the island, the rugged Nootka Indians were flourishing under far harsher conditions, as were the Kwakiutl of the north.

It was the Coast Salish Indians who inhabited the sheltered bays of the island's southeastern corner, and it was near this favoured location that the Hudson's Bay Company established Fort Victoria in 1843. The Company paid the British Crown seven shillings annually for a fur trade monopoly, and for the privilege of administering and colonizing the island.

This was the beginning of the influx of British settlers. The town of Victoria grew, eventually becoming the provincial capital in 1866, while the island's agricultural potential and natural resources such as coal, fishing and forestry, drew some of the population upcountry.

A huge portion of the island is covered in trees, from Douglas fir and hemlock to western red cedar and the soaring, age-old Sitka spruce standing in hushed groves on dank, dark valley floors. The geological heaving and glacial effects of ages past took their toll here as on the mainland, and the snow-capped peaks of the central mountain range are enormously impressive. From there, countless rivers feed the island's many lakes, then tumble toward the sea. Some of the world's best salmon fishing is found here, buoying an already thriving tourism industry.

Visitors and residents alike recognize Vancouver Island as a place of singular natural beauty. To maintain the delicate balance between a strong economy and a healthy environment will be the island's future challenge.

The Provincial Legislative Buildings in Victoria, illuminated at night.

The towering Douglas firs of Cathedral Grove on Vancouver Island.

A busy marina on Galiano Island.

A tranquil moment, canoeing in Desolation Sound.

A totem pole near Tofino on Vancouver Island's west coast.

The busy port of Tofino, a charming fishing village.

Sunset on Calvert Island just north of Vancouver Island.

Statue of Queen Victoria stands outside Victoria's Provincial Legislative Buildings, completed in 1897.

A decorative fountain at Butchart Gardens on Vancouver Island.

One of the many and varied murals at Chemainus on Vancouver Island.

Spring blossoms on a dogwood tree.

A busy fish plant at Alert Bay on Cormorant Island.

Sea kayaking near Telegraph Cove, Vancouver Island.

Thompson-Okanagan

Canada's own Garden of Eden lies midway between the Rocky Mountains and the Pacific Ocean, in the Thompson-Okanagan, where a long growing season, mild winters, and plenty of freshwater lakes and streams create ideal fruit-growing conditions. The seeds were sown in 1859, when Father Charles Marie Pandosy established his mission on the shores of Okanagan Lake and planted the first apple trees. By the turn of the century, there were over a million fruit trees in the valley, and today this region accounts for most of Canada's fruit output, from apples, pears, and plums to cherries and apricots. Also favourable to grape-growing, the region boasts many award-winning wineries. And to the north, where the valley gives way to the rolling foothills of high country, hardier vegetables plus crops of alfalfa and hay grow, and dairy farms prosper.

The lush valleys, picturesque orchards and vineyards of the north and central Okanagan are interspersed with shimmering lakes, including Okanagan Lake — the largest vestige of the glaciers of 10,000 years past. The name Okanagan, given by the Interior Salish Indians, means "treacherous water," and their legend of the lake monster, Ogopogo, is very much alive

Left: *A prolific apple tree in an orchard near Osoyoos.*

today in the minds of the imaginative. Long, hot summers are as good for tourism as they are for agriculture, and visitors flock annually to the lake country's many resorts. In keeping with the land's natural diversity, the bucolic charms of the valley and the turquoise calm of the lake country is occasionally interrupted by a towering mountain such as Big White, a popular ski resort boasting a height of 2,317 metres and an annual snowfall of over 550 centimetres. And near Osoyoos in the south, a scorchingly arid region — part of the Great Basin Desert of Oregon and Nevada — is home to cactus, sagebrush, rattlesnakes and painted turtles.

The ghost towns near Princeton are the legacy of a romantic past sitting as plaintive reminders of the wild days of the gold rush. Beginning in 1858, thousands of fortune-seekers streamed into towns like Granite City which, by 1885, was "the biggest, gaudiest mining camp in the province." Other towns, such as Coalmont, Tulameen, and Blakeburn were booming mining towns in the early 1900s, but now lie eerily quiet. There are still nuggets of gold to be found in the once-rich streams in these hills, but the true riches of this area — the beauty of the land itself and its welcoming climate — are far easier to find.

Historic O'Keefe Ranch in Vernon, built in 1867.

Water recreation on the Okanagan River at Penticton.

A grain field near Vernon, B.C.

The S.S. Sicamous, *a paddlewheeler docked at Penticton.*

Flowering orchards near Naramata, B.C.

Robert Dow Reid's "Sails" sculpture,
City Park, Kelowna.

Beach near Kelowna on Okanagan Lake.

Kootenays

In British Columbia's southeastern corner, the Rocky Mountains form a dramatic backdrop to a series of smaller mountain ranges cascading westward. Here, jagged peaks share the sky with the clouds, and valleys plunge so abruptly that some receive almost no winter sun. Glacial lakes quietly mirror forested slopes, while the region's two great river systems — the Kootenay and the Columbia — follow their tortuous routes, meeting twice before reaching the Pacific Ocean.

The original inhabitants — the Kootenay Indian Band — found protection from the outside world here, and the explorers and fur-traders of the early 19th century were hard-pressed to find a route through the forbidding terrain. It was the fortune-seekers of the 1850s gold rush who eventually linked the area — and its awesome mineral wealth — to waiting world markets.

Many present-day towns and transportation routes owe their existence to that era of economic expansion. By 1900, the once-remote Kootenays were the country's richest source of silver, gold, lead, and later, copper. Today, much of the earth's riches have been exhausted, and there remain only a few

Left: *Mount Robson, at 3954 m, is the highest peak in B.C.'s Rockies.*

prosperous mines in the area, such as the recently modernized Cominco plant in Trail.

There is no mining legacy more famous, however, than the Kettle Valley Railway. Constructed just before the turn of the century to connect the prosperous Kootenays with the coast, this railroad was an engineering miracle, literally built over and through a treacherous wall of mountains. Tunnels cut from sheer rock faces and towering trestles that once shook under the weight of mineral-laden locomotives now stand silently — a proud reminder of a great period of British Columbia's history.

The people of today's Kootenays no longer live in the dramatically remote outposts of yesteryear, but there is still a spirit of cheerful independence at work in its towns and pocket settlements. Many nationalities are represented here, from Italians and Chinese, to Russian Doukhobors. Their colourful influence, combined with the region's rich heritage and spectacular wilderness setting, have brought the hospitality and recreation industries to the fore.

St. Peter's Anglican Church on Windermere Lake in the Rockies.

Mountain goats on Mount Huber in Yoho National Park.

Glacial waters in Yoho National Park near the Alberta border.

Kimberley, ''the Bavarian City of the Rockies.''

Wildflowers bloom in alpine meadows at Mount Revelstoke National Park.

Cathedral Mountain in Yoho National Park.

Farmland near Dunster.

The railway cuts through the mountains near Field, B.C.

The fertile Creston Valley, south of Kootenay Lake.

Fort Steele is a restored turn-of-the-century mining town.

Spectacular Takakkaw Falls at Yoho National Park.

The crystal clear waters of Lake O'Hara.

A winter scene at Emerald Lake, Yoho National Park.

Cariboo-Chilcotin

In the centre of the province's interior lies the Cariboo-Chilcotin region, so named for the mountain range to its east and the native Indian band who originally inhabited its central plateau.

At the foot of the Cariboo Mountains, evergreen forests abound, and in winter the snowfall is measured in metres. Further west, the forests become sparser, the climate drier, until the mighty Fraser River cuts its powerful swath southward. Westward, between the Fraser River and the Coast Mountains stretches the Chilcotin — a plateau of gently rolling country marked by deep river gorges, rippling grasslands, myriad lakes and, here and there, the rising domes of ancient volcanoes.

The Chilcotin Indians roamed this countryside for centuries, fishing, hunting, gathering, and trading with the coastal Bella Coola Band, before Europeans penetrated the area. In 1793, Alexander Mackenzie trekked across the Chilcotin, having abandoned his water route at the perilous Fraser Canyon, and found his way to the coast over ancient Indian trails. Thereafter, the Hudson's Bay Company plied its fur trade throughout the region, but it was the gold rush of the mid-nineteenth century that really sparked development here.

Left: *Rugged terrain near Cache Creek.*

The inexorable search for gold had led would-be prospectors further and further north up the Fraser River until 1859, when colossal riches were discovered in the Cariboo near Barkerville. Suddenly, towns swelled and age-old Indian footpaths became well-worn roads, as thousands flooded the area, and frenzied miners weighed their finds not in ounces but in pounds.

For a while, this was the hub of the province. Barkerville was said to be the biggest — and was certainly the bawdiest — town north of San Francisco. The peak of this period was short-lived, but it was enough to open up the area. As individual prospecting gave way to mining companies and their hydraulic equipment, communities began to stabilize. Savvy cattlemen who had driven their herds towards the Cariboo's huge new market began to establish ranches on the grasslands, and today cattle-ranching joins mining, forestry, and tourism as the region's economic mainstays.

Central to its prosperity are the area's two largest towns, both perched at the edge of the Fraser River. Quesnel, begun as a roadhouse en route to the gold fields, now bustles with lumber and pulp mills. And further south, Williams Lake, originally by-passed by the gold rush route, didn't come to life until the railway reached it in 1919. First a cattle town, it has since benefited from many forestry and mining developments, and is now the nerve centre of the Cariboo-Chilcotin.

For all their vitality, however, these towns are forever eclipsed by the magic of the Cariboo-Chilcotin's boundless horizons and rugged terrain. It is undeniably B.C.'s land of the "big sky."

An elegant little church at Cache Creek.

Prosperous farmland near Kamloops.

A tranquil stretch of the Thompson River.

The Fraser River near Prince George.

Ranch country near Little Fort in the Cariboo.

The North

Beyond the Cariboo-Chilcotin lie the northern reaches of the province. The power of nature dominates and isolates this region, yet the land's riches have been seducing travellers for centuries.

The craggy peaks of the Rockies subside eastward into undulating foothills before flattening into the great northern plain, and the Peace River system drains into the Mackenzie River and the Arctic Ocean. Westward the great Skeena, Nass and Stikine rivers flow through a series of mountain ranges and interior plateaus, carving lush valleys as they near the Pacific. The peaks of the Coast Mountains jut out from under blankets of glaciers before they plunge into frigid ocean waters in a series of erratic inlets. And across the far northern interior, a vast expanse of lakes and rivers stretch toward the tundra.

These enormous rivers dominated the history of the region, as the lifeblood of the native Indian tribes whose livelihood depended on fishing, and as the only transportation routes for those early European pioneers who sought access to the fur pelts and gold fields of the interior.

Alexander Mackenzie was the first white man to navigate the Peace River

Left: *Dramatic contours of the Spectrum mountain range.*

in 1793. Ever since then, mankind has been harvesting the land's riches. Natural stores of fossil fuels in "the Peace," as well as two large hydro-electric dams, have made Fort St. John "the province's energy capital," while jade, argillite, asbestos, sulphur and potash are found in the west. And, of course, the most abundant resource of all, the forests, support the province's number one industry.

The economic development of these northern regions took place only after highways made them accessible to the rest of the province. The Alaska Highway, linking northern B.C. with Alaska, opened for year-round travel in 1949. And the Yellowhead Highway, running from the province's eastern border to the coast, traverses the central lake district where glacial deposits and fossil beds abound. The highway follows ancient trade routes and is marked by centuries-old Indian villages and battle sites.

Native culture is very much alive throughout the north, from that of the Carrier nation of the interior to the coastal Tsimshians and the Tlingits. But nowhere are the echoes of ancient native societies more pronounced than on the Queen Charlotte Islands. Here, first-growth red cedars up to 1,200 years old tower in lush rain forests where abandoned Haida villages lie, and faded, crumbling totems reflect a noble past. Today, native Indians continue to convey through their artistry their deep respect for their homeland.

Although man has made his presence known here, the northern third of B.C. remains a largely untouched wilderness. The Peace River District provides a safe haven for moose, elk, grizzly and black bears, the rare stone sheep, and many others, while provincial parks in the northwest, such as Atlin, Boya Lake and Spatsizi Plateau, offer opportunities for truly remote wilderness adventure. Northern B.C. remains, in Mackenzie's own words — "a magnificent theatre of nature."

Intertidal life on South Moresby Island in the Queen Charlottes.

Weathered Haida totems on Anthony Island in the Queen Charlottes.

Nootka roses blooming near the Bulkley Valley.

Foxtail barley growing in the grain fields near Dawson Creek.

The Kemano River cuts a swath through the northern Coast Mountains.

Forested slopes plunge into a northern lake near Kemano.

The Alaska Highway near Pink Mountain.

The undulating countryside of the Peace River District.

Sunset at Digby Island near Prince Rupert.

PHOTO CREDITS

Michael E. Burch pp. 1, 5, 10, 11, 13, 15, 16, 17, 18, 22, 24, 25, 26, 28, 31, 36, 39, 40, 47, 50, 54, 60, 62, 65, 67, 74, 75, 77

Bob Herger pp. 2, 32, 34, 35, 37, 38, 43, 81, 82

J.A. Kraulis pp. 33, 41, 49, 59, 63, 78, 88

Gunter Marx p. 42

Jurgen Vogt pp. 6, 9, 12, 14, 19, 20, 21, 23, 27, 44, 48, 51, 52, 53, 58, 61, 64, 66, 68, 69, 70, 73, 76, 83, 84, 85, 86, 87, 89